THIS WALKER BOOK BELONGS TO:

_____

_____

_____

_____

For Bill H. and Gerry H.
R. H. H.

For Lindsey Rae, Lacey, Trish and Ray
M. E.

FOR THE CHILDREN AND TEACHERS AT THE CAMBRIDGE-ELLIS SCHOOL
M. E. and R. H. H.

THANK YOU TO THE CHILDREN, BABIES, PARENTS AND GRANDPARENTS
Maddie, Zack, Bonnie, Paul and Lilla;
Emma, Sam, Karen and Bill;
Anita, Anthony, Lea, Ricky and Rosa

THANK YOU TO PARENTS, TEACHERS, DOCTORS AND FRIENDS
Sarah Birss, MD, Deborah Chamberlain, Ben Harris, Bill Harris, David Harris,
Gerald Hass, MD, Robyn Heilbrun, Ellen Kelly, Penelope Leach, PhD,
Elizabeth Levy, Steven Marans, PhD, Linda C. Mayes, MD, Nancy Meyer,
Anne Murphy, Janet Patterson, Carol Sepkowski, PhD, Karen Shorr,
Julie Stephenson, Pam Zuckerman, MD

First published 2000 by Walker Books Ltd
87 Vauxhall Walk, London SE11 5HJ

This edition published 2001

2 4 6 8 10 9 7 5 3 1

Text © 2000 BEE Productions, Inc.
Illustrations © 2000 Michael Emberley

This book has been typeset in Nueva

Printed in Hong Kong

British Library Cataloguing in Publication Data:
a catalogue record for this book is
available from the British Library

ISBN 0-7445-8226-1

HI NEW BABY!

written by
Robie H. Harris

illustrated by
Michael Emberley

WALKER BOOKS
AND SUBSIDIARIES
LONDON • BOSTON • SYDNEY

I'll never ever forget the moment you met your new baby brother. "Oh!" you said. "Oh!" is all you said. You didn't say anything else. But you stared at the baby – for a very long time. Then the baby wiggled his nose, sneezed and yawned. But he didn't wake up.

"That baby doesn't do anything!" you said at last. "That baby's so tiny. Its nose is so tiny. And it's still sleeping. I wish it would wake up!"

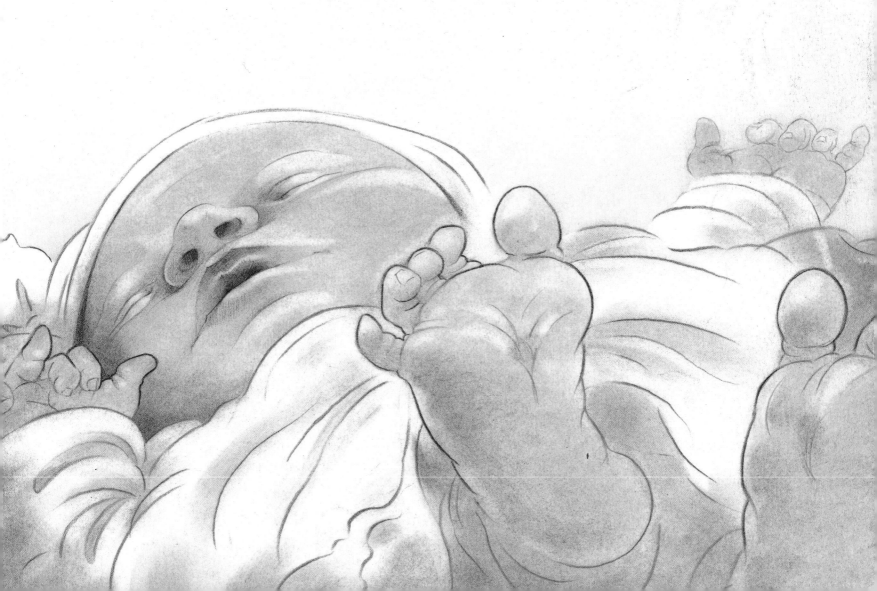

Then you touched the baby's nose with your finger. And he woke up, opened his mouth wide – and began to cry! And you covered your ears with your hands as fast as you could.

Mummy picked the baby up and
cuddled him tight.
"It's crying! It's too noisy!"
you said in a loud voice.
"Make it stop, Daddy!"

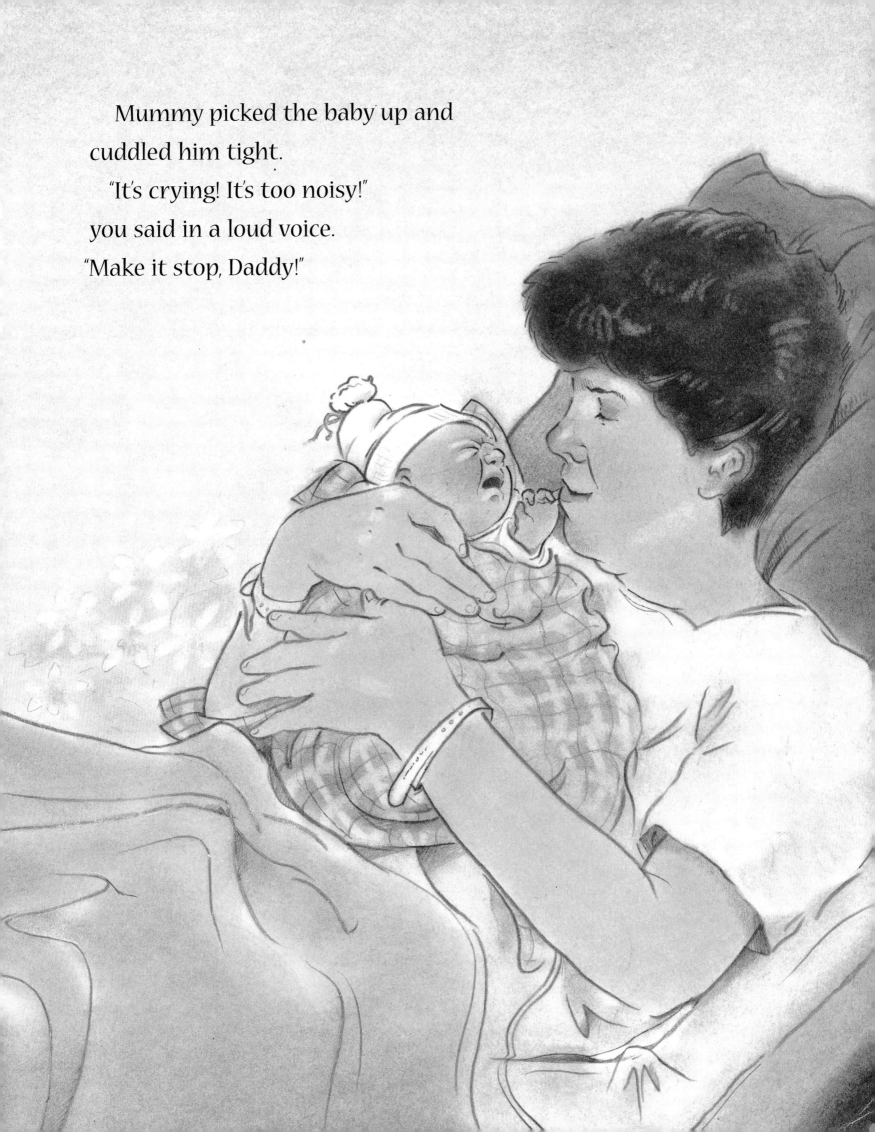

You quickly climbed on to my lap.
"I do not like that baby!" you whispered.

"But I bet he'll like having a big sister,"
I whispered back. And I gave you a hug
and a kiss.

I cuddled you, and you cuddled your
teddy bear. I loved holding you snug in
my arms. You still fitted in my lap. But
you certainly weren't a baby any more.

Soon the new baby stopped crying
and fell asleep again.

"I've seen the baby," you whispered
to me, "so let's go home now!"
And we did.

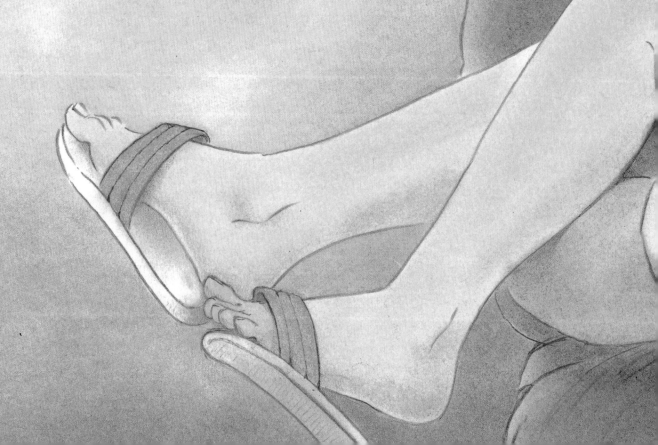

The next morning, you and I brought Mummy and the baby home. While they had a nap, we ate a piece of Grandma's cake - our favourite - even though it was still morning.

"I was never as tiny as that new baby!" you said.

"You were tiny too," I told you, "but that was a long time ago."

"I don't remember when I was a baby," you said.

"Oh, you were the most WONDERFUL baby!" I said.

"But now you're big," I told you. "Now you're our big girl."

"I'm not that big!" you shouted, as you grabbed your teddy bear and hugged it tight. Then you gave your bear a kiss on its nose.

"I've got a baby too," you said. "My bear is my baby. And my bear is much more fun than your baby!"

"I like your baby a lot!" I told you.

"I'm going to show Mummy my baby!" you said. And you ran off to show her.

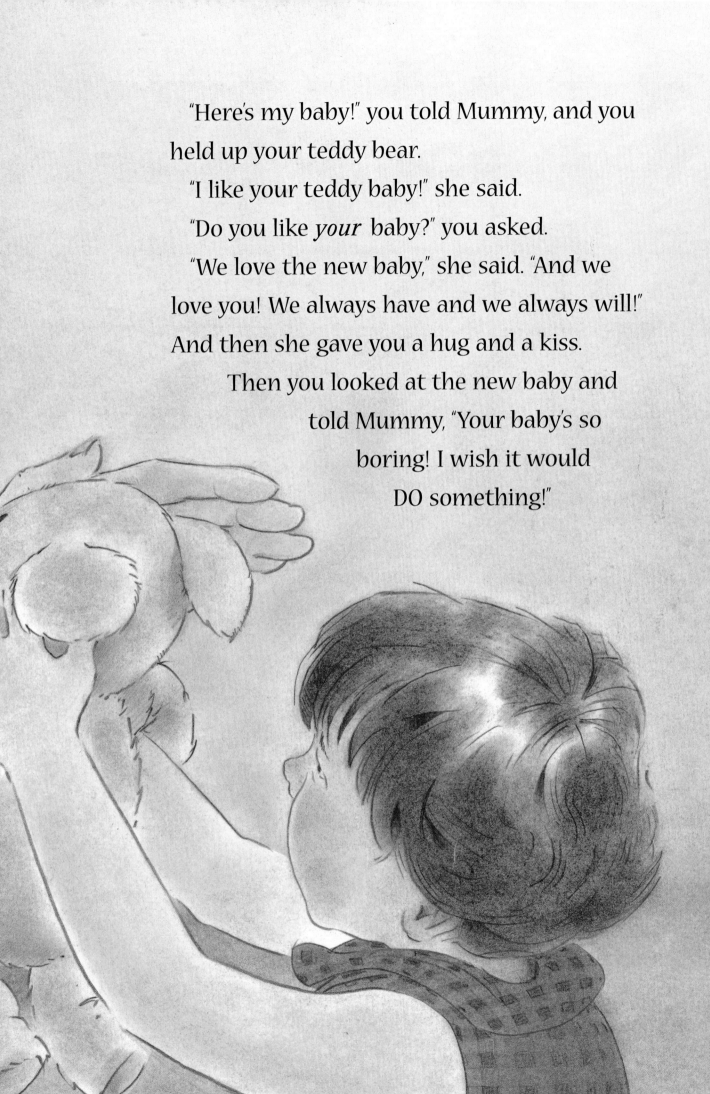

"Here's my baby!" you told Mummy, and you
held up your teddy bear.

"I like your teddy baby!" she said.

"Do you like *your* baby?" you asked.

"We love the new baby," she said. "And we
love you! We always have and we always will!"
And then she gave you a hug and a kiss.

Then you looked at the new baby and
told Mummy, "Your baby's so
boring! I wish it would
DO something!"

Suddenly, the baby began to cry again. You muttered, "Crybaby!"

"The baby's hungry," I told you. "That's why he's crying."

"I'm hungry too!" you cried. You and I ate toasted cheese sandwiches with pickles in the middle. Mummy fed the new baby, and ate a pickle. Then the new baby burped up.

"That baby is icky!" you said. "I never spit up! And I can feed myself. That baby can't!"

Then you grabbed the new baby's hat off the kitchen table – and put the hat on your head. It sat on the tippy-tippy top! It fitted – but only just!

"See, Daddy!" you shouted as you pointed to the hat. "Now *I'm* the baby!"

"See, Mummy!" you shouted as you pointed to the hat again. "Now *I'm* the baby in this family! And one baby is enough!"

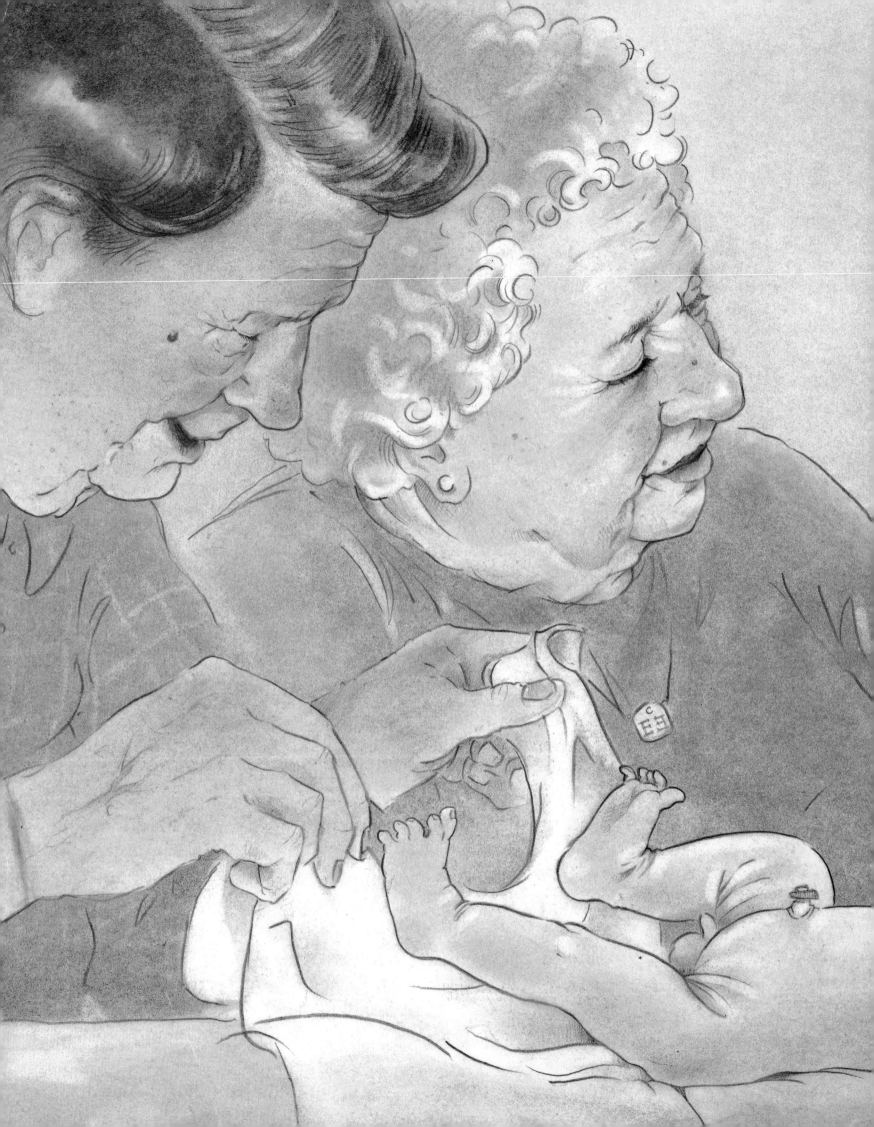

Later, when Grandma and Grandpa came to visit, the baby began to hiccup. Grandma held him over her shoulder, and you patted the baby's back. The baby burped up. Then he dribbled. Then he spit up again. Then you watched Grandpa change the baby's nappy. "That baby is yucky!" you said. "It wees in a nappy. I wee in the toilet! That baby can't!" you told me.

Then the baby looked at you – and yawned.

"That baby doesn't have any teeth!" you said. "I have so many teeth. And I can brush all my teeth. That baby can't!"

Then you smiled at the baby, opened your mouth wide and showed him all your teeth. The baby opened his mouth wide too – just like you. But he began to cry.

"I don't cry all the time like that baby does!" you said.

"That's because YOU are a big sister," I told you.

"And he's only a little baby," you said.

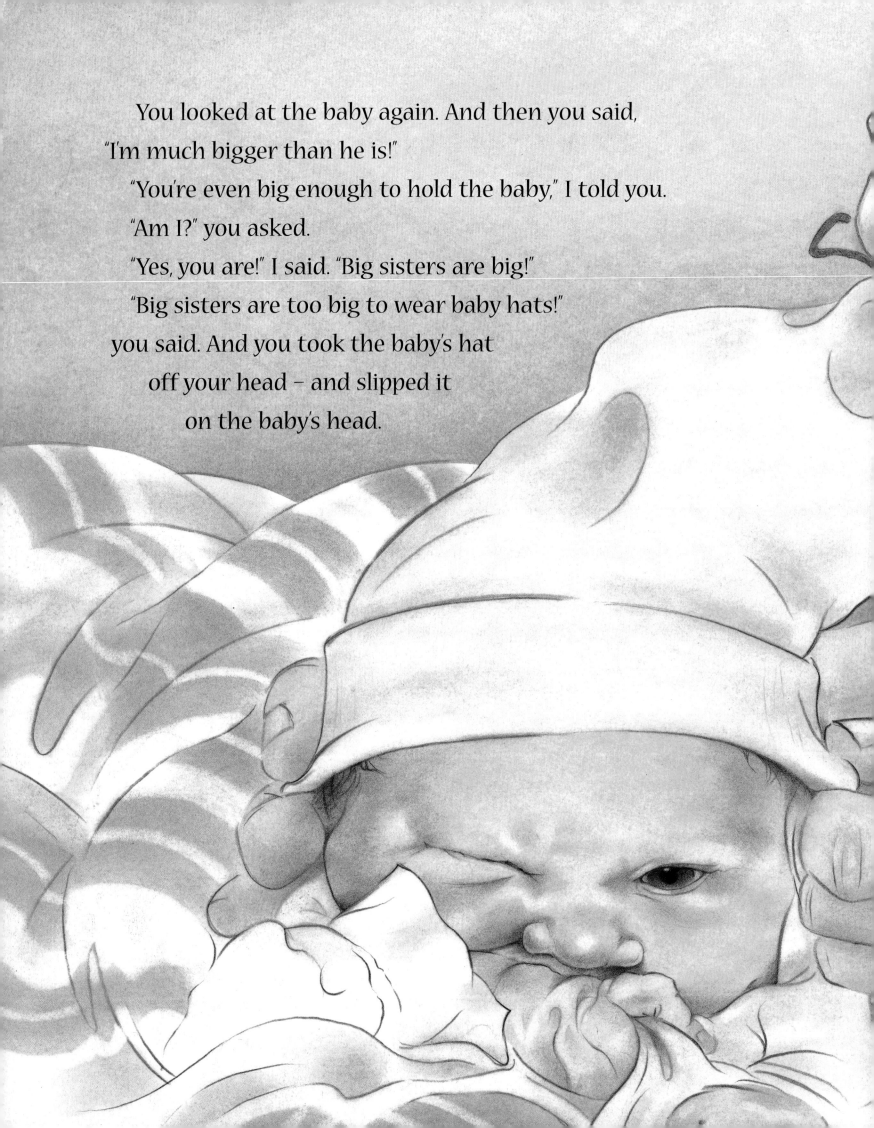

You looked at the baby again. And then you said,
"I'm much bigger than he is!"

"You're even big enough to hold the baby," I told you.

"Am I?" you asked.

"Yes, you are!" I said. "Big sisters are big!"

"Big sisters are too big to wear baby hats!"
you said. And you took the baby's hat
off your head – and slipped it
on the baby's head.

"Hi new baby!" you whispered. And the baby looked up at you – and stopped crying! I put the baby in your lap, and you rocked him in your arms. You looked so big. He looked so little.

"YOU are the baby in this family!" you whispered to him. "And one baby is enough!" Then you gave him a kiss on his nose. Soon the baby fell fast asleep.

"I like the baby quiet," you whispered. And soon you fell fast asleep too.

ROBIE H. HARRIS was inspired to write **Hi New Baby!** by her memory of the day her first child met his new baby brother. "He was both excited and disappointed, surprised that the baby was so tiny, upset when the baby cried, angry that he was no longer the baby and so proud when he could make the baby stop crying."

Robie H. Harris is also the author of *Happy Birth Day!* – the story of a child's first day in the world – and the groundbreaking international bestsellers *Let's Talk About Sex* and *Let's Talk About Where Babies Come From*, all illustrated by Michael Emberley. Robie lives in Massachusetts, USA.

MICHAEL EMBERLEY says of illustrating *Hi New Baby!*, "After carpeting my studio floor with hundreds of sketches in my struggle to capture the complex emotions of the young girl in this book, I think I finally know what must have been going on in my sister's mind on the day I was born."

Michael Emberley's parents wrote and illustrated children's books, and he produced his own first book when he was just nineteen. A keen racing cyclist, Michael has travelled extensively around the world. He now lives in Massachusetts, USA.